JACKIE CARREIRA is an award-winning writer, musician, designer, and co-founder of QuirkHouse Theatre Company. She grew up in Hackney, East London and lived in all kinds of damp and noisy flats on the North Side of the river for two thirds of her life. She also spent part of her early childhood in Lisbon's Old Quarter in the smallest flat of all with her grandparents. These colourfully diverse cities have always had a big influence on both her writing and general view of the world.

Today Jackie lives in the much gentler English county of Suffolk with an actor, two cats and more books than she has time to read. She hopes to stay there for the last third of her life. Jackie spends a lot of time in public libraries, where there are even more books. Since childhood, she has asked an annoyingly large number of questions. Not everybody likes it.

This is her first published collection of short stories.

BY THE SAME AUTHOR

NOVELS
Sleeping Through War *(Matador)*
The Seventh Train *(Matador)*

ANTHOLOGIES (as contributor)
QuirkHouse 5 *(QuirkHouse Books)*
This is Lockdown *(Kyrosmagica Publishing)*

STAGE PLAYS
Mari*
Talking In the Library* *(QuirkHouse Books)*
The Seventh Train *(Kenneth Branagh Award for New Drama)*
Winter Tails I, II and III
- Regret Rien* *(Kenneth Branagh Award for New Drama)*
Changing Rooms*
Invisible Irene *(INK Festival, Suffolk and London)*
Self Centre*

(text and performance rights available from www.lazybeescripts.co.uk)*

More information on the author can be found at
www.jackiecarreira.co.uk

For more information on cover artist, Andrea Kennard
www.flickr.com/photos/dreadwear/

THE AMBER LIBRARY

 AND OTHER STORIES

by JACKIE CARREIRA

This is a Signed Limited
First Edition

No. 86 of 125

Jackie
C x

This collection first published in Great Britain in 2022

Printed in England by Biddles Books Ltd, Norfolk, UK

ISBN: 978 1915292 421

A catalogue record for this book is available from the British Library.

THE AMBER LIBRARY

 AND OTHER STORIES

by JACKIE CARREIRA

This book is dedicated to my husband, AJ Deane,
who has never once believed that I couldn't do all
the things I only dreamed I could.

And for my mother and grandmothers, and all the
dreams that were kept from them.
I will try to live some of them for you.

And to the generosity of Andrea Kennard.
A little bit of Amber for my Ruby Topaz friend.

"There is no greater agony than bearing
an untold story inside you."
- Maya Angelou -

"A word after a word after a word
is power."
- Margaret Atwood -

CONTENTS

INTRODUCTION

There were no books in our house when I was growing up. My parents were immigrants to Britain, moving to London from Portugal in the early 1960s in search of a better life. As it is for most immigrants, this was far tougher than they had envisaged. And so, books were a luxury that my parents could not afford.

That's not strictly true. There were six books in our house: A large encyclopaedia of cars and motorbikes that belonged to my brother; a book of Fairy Tales that was a gift from my (not fairy) godmother; a volume containing the first half of the letter 'A' from the *Encyclopaedia Britannica* (left behind by a door-to-door salesman who must have believed my father would buy the rest if he returned. He was wrong); two *Readers Digest* hardback editions that came free with something or other (*The Old Curiosity Shop* by Charles Dickens, and a biography of Victorian actress Ellen Terry. I'm pretty sure I was the only family member to ever have opened either of them, let alone read them!); and a thick, well-thumbed Portuguese cookbook that my mother had brought with her when she came to England. This one looked like it had once belonged to *her* mother. Possibly even her grandmother.

This random collection of books was my first little library, and I read them all, even the cookbook. Today our house is full of books, as if I'm still trying to make up for the lack of them as a child. My growing collection is just as eclectic as it was back then. From William Blake to Benjamin Zephaniah, George Eliot to Margaret Atwood, HG Wells to Kurt Vonnegut, José Saramago to John Steinbeck.... and on and on. Too many to list here.

The one thing my favourite authors have in common is that they tell human stories. They show me things about people, and I understand the world and myself a little more with each one.

This book - my first collection of short stories and poetry - attempts to do the same, and is equally eclectic. They are snapshots of human life, of despair and hope, of loss and love, inspiration and acceptance.

So, dear reader, you may start wherever you need to in this book in order to either see the struggle or seek the antidote. Your choice. You'll find both within. I hope you recognise something of yourselves and your lives in these stories, as I do.

For every high there is a low. For every 'yes' there is a 'no'. The task for each human being is to walk the fine line in between and see both desolation and elation for the imposters that they are. Somewhere in the middle is an indefatigable human spirit. Somewhere, in each story, is the same.

Jackie Carreira
Suffolk, 2022

ABOUT THE OYSTER

There once was an oyster that had no pearl. It had no pearl because it could not stand the grit. And because it could not stand the grit, it kept itself away from everything in the ocean, or on the shore, or falling from the sky, that might cause the grit to enter the safety of its shell.

Because of this, the oyster never came to know the beauty of the pearl that is created, first from knowing and then overcoming the grit.

PULLING OFF PETALS

It is two days since the Revolution. The song has been playing on the radio ever since; the voice of the singer carrying the hearts and minds of the people. That's what the announcer said. Everybody's listening to it. The song carries their hopes, fears, dreams, and the song seems to fill the whole of our apartment into every dusty corner. In the tightly packed streets of the Old Town the music dances along the pavements and climbs up the tall, skinny buildings stuffed with homes. The sound echoes and bounces off tiles and stone walls, and it runs down the narrow street, rushing over grey cobble stones like water through the drains.

Clean washing flaps and claps time in the breeze, hanging from thick, plastic ropes strung across the windows. The air is filled with the odour of old beer, wet linen and the city's ancient sewage system – rarely unblocked and hardly noticed by the residents most days. On the patchwork façade of the buildings, window boxes bulge with young tomato plants and spring flowers, and their rich scent sits on the others like expensive perfume on a wet dog.

My small, square bedroom window lets in the music and the voices and the smells; all so familiar, yet everything is different today. I sit on the dark, wooden floor without my shoes on and notice, for the first time, that my feet are moving unconsciously in time with the music from outside. I make it conscious and add my hands to the dance, just to enjoy it for a moment or two.

Last week I danced with the others. It's Saturday morning, and I should be at the Youth Movement meeting today. But there isn't any Youth Movement meeting this week. There will never be a Youth Movement again. It was abolished yesterday – the day after the revolution.

I take my uniform down from the brass hook on the back of the bedroom door and carefully lay it out on the bed. I let my hand stroke the brown, woollen skirt, smoothing out the creases from last week's parade, then gently do up the top button of the green, serge shirt. I pick up the brown beret and run my thumb along the coloured piping all around the edge – the colours of the flag. The colours are still the same today, aren't they? I don't know if the colours will change tomorrow.

I turn to the back of my closed bedroom door to the mirror that the uniform had been hiding, force my thick, unruly brown hair behind my ears and place the beret carefully on my head, just like I did last week. How can the girl in the glass look the same when everything has changed? I thought it would show on my face.

Yesterday Isabel had a uniform just like mine. We were both picked to be members of the Youth Movement when we were eleven years old. She was already taller than me, and I know all the boys think she's prettier, but mother says I'm smarter and that makes up for it. Sometimes I choose to believe her. After we were chosen, our teacher made us stand in front of the class in our uniforms so that all the other children could see the clever girls. Only the brightest or the most athletic were picked to be in the Youth Movement. Only the most special would represent their generation at parades and special events; even the President's birthday. And we did feel special that day. I have to admit that, at least to myself. We were part of the elite – the future of a once great nation, charged with making it great again. What does it mean now? Is the future still in our hands? My hands look so small.

I think that maybe Isabel has forgotten that day. It was three years ago, but I remembered it every time I placed the brown beret on my head. Every meeting, every parade I remembered. I try to smooth the creases out of the green, serge shirt and hold it up in front of my chest and look in the mirror... I thought the revolution was meant to get rid of the bad things, but not this. How could this be bad? The revolution was meant to take away the poverty and the oppression. It was meant to remove the hated secret police whose name parents would invoke to frighten naughty children and silence feuds with neighbours. But not this, surely.

Yesterday I sat in Isabel's bedroom and watched as she took her mother's dressmaking shears to the brown wool and the green serge and laughed. Before that we had listened in the kitchen to the man on the radio while we drank celebratory hot chocolate and ate cinnamon biscuits. The man on the radio had told everyone that it was over. He said it again and again, getting louder and shriller as the passion poured out of his mouth. 'The people's army have won and the old regime is gone,' he said. 'It's over.' He said that the revolution was going 'to give the people back that freedom of which they had for so long been deprived.' Isabel's father had cheered and beat the air with his fists. He poured himself a glass of whisky and drank to the future and to health. After his second glass, he sent me and Isabel to her bedroom to play.

'We're free!' Isabel said. 'Do you know what that means? We can do anything we like.'

'Like what?' I asked.

'Like this,' she said, and with one smooth slice Isabel cut her green, serge shirt in half, straight up the back, and laughed with impish excitement.

I was scared. 'We'll get into trouble,' I said.

Isabel thought my fear was funny. 'In trouble from who?' she said. 'My mother gave me the shears herself.'

There was a small, gilt framed picture of the Virgin on Isabel's bedside table. A gift from her grandmother. I'd seen it many times before, but now I looked at it as if I was quietly begging absolution for my friend's behaviour. The blue-veiled lady looked back at me with sad, patient eyes and I touched my thumb and forefinger to my forehead, chest, both shoulders and then lips, to try and kiss the fear away. *What if it goes wrong?* I thought. *What if they take it all back?* Isabel didn't notice the small sacrament of penance going on beside her as the blades slid next through the brown skirt and then through the yellow cotton tie with the green trim that was lying, neatly ironed, next to the fragments of green fabric. What had once made her special was nothing but second-hand ribbons.

Today, as a treat, Isabel's father is going to take her to see the tanks that have lined up in the main square. He was there last night and said that the tanks were covered in red carnations. The people had brought the soldiers gifts of wine and food and taken photographs as the soldiers sat on the tanks next to pretty girls. By now, me and Isabel should be making our way to the school yard to practise for Our Lady's parade in May. But there is no Youth Movement meeting today.

There is a gentle knock on my door and I take the beret off and put it back on the bed with the green, serge shirt. Mother opens the door before I can say anything. I know that she just wants to check on me. The sound of the radio from the kitchen where my father sits grows louder and I can hear the excited voice of yet another commentator on the radio. There must be a queue of them waiting to speak. They must have been holding their tongues for so long that they're all stuffed with too many words. I hadn't noticed it before.

'I'm going to work now, Ana,' my mother says. Then her voice goes soft. 'Are you okay?'

I just nod and smile. Then my mother sees the uniform and tries to understand. I know because I can see it on her face. Then I tell her that Isabel had destroyed her uniform the day before. She asks me if that's why it's on the bed and I tell her that I don't know. She had worn the same Youth Movement costume at my age but had lost her pride in it a long time ago. She had been a child and then a woman in the 'New State'. Now she was a mother in a new world. Her daughter would not have to be careful who she spoke to and what she said. I would have opportunities that she could only have dreamed of. I could have a real education now. I would be able to do anything I wanted with my future. She told me all of this while we sat on the bed next to my uniform. I want her hopes and dreams to be mine. I want all those things but I didn't know how to say it, so I just said: 'Yes, I know.'

Then my mother leaves the room. I thought that was the end, but then she returns with her own dressmaking shears clutched in her hand. The big blades glint for a second when the morning sun shining through the window hits the metal.

She hands them to me with a grown-up kind of smile and leaves the room to go to work, closing the door behind her.

The shears are clean and sharp. I can feel the cold weight of them in my hand. I place them carefully on the bed and open the bottom drawer of my dressing table. Inside, at the back, is a neat, square bundle wrapped in blue tissue paper. I open it and lay my holy communion dress out next to the uniform. It had been made by my mother's own hands; cut from yards of white, cotton lace with the same dressmaking shears.

I look at the odd collection of clothes, flat and empty, then wrap them both together in the same blue tissue paper and place them again at the back of the drawer. I pick up the shears and go to find my father. He is in the kitchen listening to the same song on the radio. Nobody seems to want to hear anything else.

'Ana,' he says, 'Do you want to come down to the square to see the tanks? Your mother said Isabel will be there.' He looks younger today. I've never seen my father look like a boy before. Perhaps we don't want to believe our parents were children once. I smile at him and he smiles right back. 'Come on,' he says, 'don't you want to come and see the revolution?'

'Yes,' I say. But he knows me better than that.

'It's okay, Ana,' he says. 'It's over.'

I try to form the question in my mind before I say the words out loud. My father sees the struggle, gets up from his chair and takes my hand. 'What if it's not over?' I say. He squeezes my fingers and his feel cool. 'What if it all comes back someday?' I ask. 'What if they want it all back in the future and punish us for today?'

My father lets my hand go, lifts my chin and looks me squarely in the eye, as if to insist that I see him as clearly as possible when he speaks. 'Listen, Ana. The future is up to you. It starts today, right now. You can stride bravely towards it, or walk backwards in fear. What do you choose?'

'Can I take some time to decide?' I ask.

He laughs and lets me go. 'Ana, my Ana. If I offered you meat and potatoes you'd ask for lemonade. Now, are you ready to come outside with me to see the revolution?'

'Yes,' I say.

'Good!' he says. 'This is history, my girl. And let's hope you never have to see another revolution in your lifetime,' then he switches off the radio and urges me to move with a tilt of his head towards the door.

'Okay,' I say. 'I'll just put these away first.' I open my mother's sewing basket and slip the shears inside.

NO TIME AT ALL

It's been seven weeks. That's no time at all. Everything's happened to me as if I wasn't there. It's like some kind of conveyor belt. I can see everything moving past me in all its detail, but there's no sound that fits. Someone turned the volume off seven weeks ago and replaced it with white noise. That's what it feels like.

'Get away for a bit,' my sister said. 'You just need some time. We'll take care of the cats.' I just nodded the same slow nod I had given for everything else.

Now I'm walking alone through the gates in the early morning mist, waiting for my first glimpse of what we always talked about seeing together. At first it feels like I shouldn't have come, like I'm doing this behind her back. I try to convince myself that I'm doing it for her, but it doesn't work so I just keep walking.

The first thing I notice is that the sound is different. Yesterday in Delhi all I could hear out of the white noise was the people chattering and pulling at me for money, but it just floated past on that conveyor belt. They don't let the hawkers and beggars come in here. Their jostle and chatter is replaced by the sound of parakeets and monkeys playing in the trees.

I walk along the red paved pathway and hardly notice the pristine gardens and geometrically cut lawns. There's a fusion of incense and rose petals in the air, so clean after the dust of the city. Everything in me is pulled towards the monument. It sits on a platform in front of the sky, bathed in a soft, pink glow from the early morning sun. I walk halfway towards it and there's a bench in the middle before the final approach begins. I sit for a while. Amy would have loved this.

I always thought it would be smaller somehow. It's hugely grand but so quiet and dignified. Everything about it points up to the heavens like the most beautiful, precious offering to the gods. I pull the guidebook out of my pocket and read the words:

The Taj Mahal is the greatest monument to love ever erected. Built by Shah Jahan in memory of his wife Mumtaz, it took over twenty years to build and employed twenty thousand workers...

There's more, but I close the guidebook and put it down on the bench beside me. The conveyor belt has stopped. No more white noise. The tears start to come for the first time, but no-one seems to notice this lone, weeping tourist sitting on a bench. The Taj has them, just like it has me. Its grip is soft but strong and it has the ability to stop time. I sit on the bench and let it hold me for as long as it wants.

We burnt Amy's body seven weeks ago. The cancer choked her so fast that none of us were prepared. Half her friends didn't even know until after the funeral. There was so much to do, coffins and cats and paperwork. We burnt her and I don't even know where the plaque's going to be. Maybe they told me. I can't remember now.

Amy lived for just twenty-eight years. It took that long to build the Taj Mahal. No time at all.

ESCAPE TO THE MOUNTAINS

It was as if everyone else was dead. The world, so big and busy, had shrunk to contain only him and his senses, contained and kept close inside the mountains that moulded the glen.

He sat today at the old writing desk, placed deliberately in front of the best window of the small cottage living room, the window that framed the view down the green and purple glen, dotted with stones and slashes of streams and distant waterfalls. The end of the view, at least a mile away, was closed shut by the dark, craggy peaks ahead, and the whole scene before him sloped outwards and upwards like a giant's mixing bowl. Here and there were clusters of strong, sharp grass, pointed upwards in tufts, huddled in little groups against the brave Highland winds. Then an odd flicker of white among the grass and heather would catch his eye, as a rabbit sprang to and fro before disappearing out of sight.

The loudest sound was the tin-can crackle of the open fire next to him as the orange flames licked and ate another piece of wood. And from time to time a hollow breath would blow down the chimney as the wind pushed and slapped at the cottage.

Grey-white clouds slid across the sky towards him as he watched through the window. They looked fresh and clean and new, as if this was the place of their birth. They moved beneath paler grey skies, never stopping. Never stopping. They kept coming as if they must.

Sitting at the old writing desk, he moved his legs to rest one upon the other, paused briefly then moved them again just to hear the rasp of linen on linen as he did so. He breathed a sigh, and listened to that too. For a moment he felt scared, not for himself, but for what he was not.

It was nearly a month since he'd left everything behind. He could no longer stand the emptiness inside him, the blankness in his head, the numbness of his mind. Work was unsatisfying and meaningless, serving only to pay bills, which were too large and too frequent. His siblings had moved off inside their own families and left him where he'd always been. The calls and cards were friendly but infrequent, warmed only by the fires of habit and duty.

His social life – what there was of it – was even less satisfying than work. Perhaps he had expected too much. Over the years he'd taken to filling the void by padding himself out, dabbling with drugs and alcohol in an amateur manner whenever the void grew too great. And often at those times he'd find some female to empty himself out upon, but these short intimacies only highlighted the lack of deep feeling by their very shallowness. Then, when his fill was reached, he'd stop with the drugs and drink as abruptly as he began, cursing himself for his weaknesses. The more he cursed, the greater grew his disappointment, and the more time he spent cursing the less he did about it.

Four months ago, he reached his thirty-eighth birthday. He sat in the pub that night and looked around at the people that he had chosen to celebrate this milestone with. Just acquaintances, really. Two guys from work, one of their girlfriends, and a small selection of the locals from the pub who drifted in and out of the tame celebration. Everyone talks in pubs about things they would never tell their closest families, the beer and whisky loosening their thoughts to come tumbling out of their mouths. Then they walk away into hidden lives, never sharing the daylight of themselves.

He'd come home that night not drunk, just empty, and sat for a long time on his own. He fought the urge to do anything but sit with the discomfort of himself and what he had not done for thirty-eight years, and it was in those moments of lucid impotence that he decided that enough was enough.

Endings are often more time-consuming than beginnings, and it took him three months to finish everything that he saw going nowhere. It took three months to work out his notice; three months to live out the lease on his North London flat; three months to sell or store all his accumulated superfluousness, and so it went on. The goodbyes were much quicker. A drink in the pub with whoever cared or happened to be there, and a visit to his parents, discussing family and friends that he'd mostly already forgotten.

Now he sat at the window, looking down along the glen, where he'd come to find himself. It had never occurred to him that, wherever he went, he would take what little there was of himself along too.

A month had gone by since he'd come to the cottage. It took him that long to realise that he'd escaped into another prison. Six months was the term he'd signed himself up for, and he was too stubborn to quit before that time was up. In any case, he'd paid the rent in advance and the little he'd managed to save over the years was just enough to cover food, fuel and cigarettes.

He'd thought originally that this isolated and windswept place would be where he could write that book that everyone's supposed to have in them, or that music that would make his fortune, all the songs that had been trapped inside him for years. But so far, his only produce was cigarette butts, bin bags and ash from the logs that he'd burnt his way through trying to keep himself warm.

There was no phone signal here, no electricity, no distractions except for the little black portable radio that refused to pick up anything but Radio 4. He loathed himself for starting to care about what happened in *The Archers*, and for understanding finally the calm gibberish of the *Shipping Forecast*. Once or twice, he'd managed to find some satisfaction in arguing out loud in his empty room with hypocrite politicians on late-night panel shows. Nobody would ever hear his arguments. They were futile debates into the dark, candlelit nights; nights that grew longer and darker with each passing day.

Beside the cottage was a narrow, gravelled, well-worn path that led through the glen and up into the mountains that rose over the back of the cottage. The path had been well trod by dayglo, rain-proofed walkers who filed up and down during the summer months. It was September now and the walkers had thinned to just a handful a day. He could see them coming for half a mile or so down the glen and always hid between the windows of the living room or the kitchen to avoid any kind of contact. Some of the most curious would squint through the windows shamelessly, wondering who might live in such a beautiful but isolated place. The nearest dwelling was three miles to the east, and at least ten miles in all other directions.

The walkers would move themselves from the window and pass on, slightly embarrassed at their own nosiness once they saw a discarded jacket on the armchair or a smouldering cigarette in the ashtray. Then he'd sit back at the window when he was sure that they'd passed, and watch again.

Today he found himself with a panic washing over him once the last walkers had gone. He was sorry that he hadn't come to the door and said 'hello,' or chosen that time to be outside fetching more wood from the shed so that he'd have an excuse to pass the time of day. They might have been thirsty or needed the toilet and he could have invited them in. They would have thought of him as a generous stranger on their long journey, or as the mysterious man of the glen, then he might have felt a moment of usefulness, or at least had a short conversation with another human being. He could have been anyone he'd wanted to be. How would they know? He could have made his life more interesting than theirs, if he'd wanted to.

Gripped by this strange, sorry panic he scraped his chair back across the grey nylon carpet, and ran to the door. By the time he got out to the back of the house, the walkers were disappearing round the first bend of the mountain path, pushing the ground away with their sticks, deep in a conversation too far away to hear. A gust of wind caught his face. It was cold.

He turned to walk back to the front door then stopped dead as he caught sight of the room inside his window. The sight that the curious walkers had seen. It looked too perfect, deceptively romantic with the writing desk sloping away, his ashtray, cigarettes and the fat church candle sitting on top of it. On the deep, white window sill that cut into the thick wall, stood a row of randomly-sized books, none of them read, covers curling from the damp, smoky atmosphere. In one corner of the window sill sat a small, mixed group of rocks and pebbles, picked up with some forgotten intention during his first few days here, the days when he walked and walked and explored the glen and its mountains, the wind in his eyes and the cares of the world far away. He realised now that he hadn't been out on a walk for over two weeks; hadn't even left the house except to fetch logs and kindling.

He stood and looked through that window for a long time, the damp wind slapping his hair across his face like cold, wet paper. He could see a notepad and pen on the desk, partially hidden by a week-old newspaper, read and re-read and re-read. The notepad was empty of everything except grand intentions, but the crossword on the back of the newspaper was complete.

Behind the desk against the far wall leant an acoustic guitar, looking like some forgotten ornament rather than instrument. Just part of the random collection of furniture, enough furniture for a family of four with bad taste and too much disposable income. Anyone passing might think some bohemian artist lived here. A writer or a musician, locked away in his own creativity with the magnificent glen as his muse. But when he looked in through his window, he realised that no-one lived here at all. Someone was just staying for a while for some half-reasoned reason. This was no more a home for him than it was for the walkers who only owned their personal glimpse through the window.

He imagined that he could see himself looking out, as he had done for hours. What the hell was he looking for? He'd been lonely in the city, sure, but what made him think he'd be less lonely here?

It crept up on him like a gentle nudge, but it went deep. The only thing he'd been running away from was himself, and that was the only thing he couldn't escape from. The distractions of the city were not the problem. Money and commercialism and meaningless gadgets were not the problem. He'd forgotten to have a life, that was all, and in this wild landscape, devoid of the expressions of his culture and its pettiness, he'd somehow expected to get filled up with life from the outside. It had been put aside some time long ago, perhaps in his childhood or teenage years. It had been put aside so quietly and delicately that he hadn't even noticed until now. His life wasn't in anything outside. Not even in him, very much.

It started to rain, that fine, gentle rain that lives in the Highlands. He stood at the window as the rain dripped down his hair and on to his face. He stood there until it soaked his collar. He looked into the empty room, that perfect-looking empty room. Just how he had imagined it. Just how it looked in the brochure.

Then he knew. The door of the cage was open. It always had been.

THROUGH THE MILL

I've got the rest of the week off for my troubles. It's Thursday afternoon and I'm expected behind the spindle again, first thing on Monday morning. Amelia wasn't given three days when her first one died.

I've climbed the hill that rises behind the town to the river that flows back down to it, and I stop to feel the cold water in my hands. Ma is with my other four. I've told her they must wash their hands and faces before they go to bed. I bring the fresh water up to wash my face too. It wakes up my heavy eyes and everything looks clearer.

The river looks so thin and bright. Stones and clumps of grass sit inside the water, stroked one way, washed clean and smooth. Fish and skimming flies dart here and there in the afternoon light as if they have somewhere else to be. Not like me.

How can this soft, clean river be strong enough to push that big, dirty water wheel a mile down the hill? The wheel that stops for nothing lest the governor loses profits. He'll have me under the big loom on Monday. One way or another I'll have to pay back three full days of grieving with pay.

I put my fingers back in the water and move them to and fro. By the time this water gets downhill it will be full of soot and dirt and soap to scrub the floors. It doesn't know what it's got coming. Things are so clean when they're born, before they've gone through the mill.

CONVERSATION WITH A YEW TREE

Don't leave me in the corner by the wall
where the ivy grows thick
and pushes out cracks in the stone;
where the weeds weave tangled blankets of forgetfulness.
Don't leave me naked on the grass
where the rain washes away the time;
where the wind wipes away the place,
and they both eat the letters in my name.
Don't leave me near the iron fence
where the dogs come to drop
and the wheels of cars blow plastic bags
like exhausted dancers.
But let me rest underneath your arms,
in the evergreen shade of your dignity,
and watch over me for a thousand years
so the weeds and the rain and the dirt
don't rub me out too quick.

FLIGHT OF THE FALCON
(Excerpt from an unfinished novel)

Two peregrine falcons had been spotted nesting, high up in the steeple of an old church in East Anglia, not far from Mae's little, rented house. The local paper had run a special feature with colour pictures and comments from the vicar:

'Of course,' he said, 'we wouldn't want to discourage people from coming to see the rare sight of these beautiful birds, but we would ask that visitors make every effort not to disturb them.' The Reverend Noel Smith, 49, then added, 'And when people do come, may I take the opportunity to remind them that the current Save The Steeple fund is still short by seven thousand pounds.'

Mae chose her moment carefully and arrived at the churchyard at eight o'clock on Thursday morning. The winter sun had not been up for long and it was weak, held back by thick, pale clouds. But it was dry, at least, and not as cold as it had been.

The village where the peregrines had made their nest was small but packed full of houses, some old and picturesque and painted a traditional Suffolk Pink, like the old days but created now with Heritage colours from Crown and Dulux instead of the original whitewash and pigs' blood. Most of the houses though were square and brown, squat and modern, crowded around the church with no respect for the architecture.

Most people would be leaving for work or school or shopping, thought Mae, and the churchyard would be quieter than at the weekend. It was indeed, just the sound of the last round of car engines starting up for their midweek morning duties.

Behind the church in a hotchpotch graveyard was an old oak bench. It had turned grey with age, just like people do. From there Mae could sit and get a good view of the whole building and its steeple without having to see the road behind it. She'd brought her camera with her, as well as a small sketchbook and coloured pencils so that she could, at least, get some images of the church, even if she didn't see the peregrines. Her watercolours of local churches always sold remarkably well, and Mae always wondered at this as all she kept hearing was how increasingly secular England was becoming. Why were people so interested in something they didn't believe in anymore? Perhaps old stone churches, with their stained-glass eyes, were now destined for the 'pretty, not practical' pile, like thatched roofs and water wheels and five-inch heels. Or perhaps it was just simple nostalgia.

The blackbirds had already started singing the late winter chorus, each with his own song, questioning and answering each other, hidden in the yew trees and the sycamores around the churchyard. Further away, in a field behind the new houses, a crow cut across the blackbird song with two or three loud shrieks, as if he was jealous of their melodies.

Much higher up, thin, sharp and black against the clouds, three birds circled and darted in the sky. Mae studied them, camera ready in her lap, in case they were the elusive falcons. But the tails weren't right and the silhouettes were too thin. Perhaps they were swallows. No, it was too cold for swallows. Surely, they went south for the winter? Perhaps they were stray starlings away from their flock, or maybe just some high-flying crows.

Mae switched on the camera and the digital mechanism whirred into action. She liked the shapes that the birds made in the sky as they swept across each other like a wandering trapeze act. She took a couple of pictures, decided it just didn't look as good through the lens in this light, and rested the camera back in her lap, ready still, just in case. She watched the dancing birds for a while. It was soothing for her. The car engines were now few and far between and even the crow had stopped complaining.

Mae thought about getting the sketchbook out of her bag and making some preliminary sketches of the church. The windows looked dark and gloomy in this light, but she could always go inside later, if the church was unlocked, and photograph the details of the stained glass with the daylight behind them, as they were meant to be seen. She peered at the windows across the churchyard, trying to make out the story they were trying to tell. The saint that the church was named after, perhaps. Or was it Noah and the animals, two by two?

Then suddenly there was a crack of feathers, a short, high-pitched sound, and Mae saw her. One of the peregrines flew from the top of the steeple where she'd been hiding and raced out and up above the churchyard. The blackbirds stopped their songs and a couple of pigeons that had been hiding in the yew trees scrambled and flapped out of sight, as quick as their wings could carry their fat bodies.

Mae sprang up from the bench to get a better view and the camera dropped from her lap and clattered onto the gravel at her feet. For a second, she stopped and thought to check the camera for damage, but then saw how quickly the peregrine was ascending. The camera could wait. It was no match for her eyes and she decided she didn't want to lose sight of the magnificent bird. Mae moved out from under the cover of the sycamores shading the bench and watched the creature rising higher and higher into the sky. After only four or five seconds she was no more than a shrinking dot in the sky and Mae marvelled at how fast the bird must be travelling. And then, in a blink, the peregrine disappeared. She had shot right into the pale, grey clouds and was gone. Mae held her breath for a moment, waiting for the bird to emerge again, out of the clouds and back into view, but there was nothing. Even the three black, dancing birds had gone, as if everything in the sky had cleared a path out of respect for the fastest animal on earth.

Mae spun round where she stood, checking the empty sky for the dot that was once the bird. She thought she saw her once, twice, but no, it was a trick of the light or a speck of dust or something in her eye. It had all happened too quickly. She just wanted to slow the world down for a minute and rewind, enjoy those few, brief seconds of seeing this beautiful thing; her sharp eyes and smooth head, her double-pointed tail and stiff beak, the swiftness and precision with which she moved through the air, hunting for prey.

A minute went by, then another, then five. Still there was no sign of the bird. Still the other birds kept silent. Mae was standing in the middle of the churchyard now and her camera was still lying on the gravel in front of the bench. She took one more scanning look around the sky, her eyes resting finally on the steeple. She couldn't see the other peregrine of the pair. He must be huddled down in the nest, too high for prying eyes.

Mae sighed and turned to walk back to the bench. She took two steps and froze. The peregrine was there, in the distance, straight ahead of her above the trees. She hadn't seen her drop out of the sky but there she was, no longer a black dot but close enough to see that the bird was hurtling towards her at enormous speed. She had something in her mouth. It was one of the birds that Mae had watched circling with its companions. It was a starling, hanging limp in the peregrine's beak. Although it was several feet above Mae, she instinctively ducked as the bird swooped over her and up into the steeple nest. And then she knew that the starling was dead. A hearty meal for the peregrine and her mate. Then all three of the birds were gone as if they'd never been in the sky.

It was a long minute before Mae turned again and walked back to the bench. She picked up the camera from the ground and checked it over. It was broken. The battery cover had been cracked when it dropped and the lens had a small chip on the same side. She sat on the oak bench, under the grey clouds, and watched the steeple for a long time. Suddenly all the colours in the churchyard had become muted. She didn't see the peregrine anymore. Eventually the blackbirds started to sing again.

There was no pain. No headache, no churning stomach, no shortness of breath as there usually was when Mae ventured out of the house on her own. All she felt was a kind of confused numbness. The starling was dead, torn to pieces by now by the peregrines in the steeple. When the bird had flown over her head, Mae had caught a glimpse of her eyes, fierce and sharp. But she had also seen the starling's eyes, cold and dead. He had flown with such silent grace, high above the churchyard, dancing with his companions in the sky, only to be plucked out and extinguished in a heartbeat, coldly, economically. It was horrific but so natural. She thought she knew the starling's pain, but she couldn't feel it.

Mae sat inside the numbness for as long as she could bear. She thought about the dancing starling cut down. Then she suddenly thought about her father, cut down too young. And her mother even younger. She thought about her sister and her brother, and of being alone in the churchyard on a Thursday morning, the only witness to this piece of aerial drama, and she felt a little sick. Ah, there was the familiar pain at last. Perhaps it had just been late, distracted by the birds. She felt unease moving in her stomach, slowly rising towards her chest. She gave a cough and pushed the pain up, feeling it catch in her throat. There it was, like an old dressing gown.

Mae collected her sketchpad, her pencils and the broken camera and put them all in her bag. She would get the camera fixed tomorrow. It didn't look that bad. For now, she needed to go home and find her oil pastels.

Five hours later there was a large piece of cartridge paper sitting on the floor in the middle of Mae's living room. Although the sun was now very low in the sky there was still some winter light outside, but the curtains were drawn across the windows. Mae sat folded up on the sofa, hugging her knees tightly to her chest. Her bare feet felt cold. This latest picture disturbed her. She stared at it from the safest distance possible, from the other side of the room.

The paper had moved slightly when she'd managed to move away from it and the dislodgement had left a sharp line of charcoal dust and pastel smears on the wooden floor. This had the effect of framing the picture on one side and made the dark colours on the white paper stand out even more.

It wasn't the fact of the picture's existence that bothered Mae, it was the subject matter. Over the years that it had taken to amass the produce in the trunk, she had become accustomed to abstract shapes and angry colours; shades of mess piled on top of each other with layers of fat, oily lines. None of the sellable, pretty watercolours of churches and Olde Worlde shops lived in the trunk. Only the oil pastel pictures were shut away there. The ones that no-one was meant to see. But this picture was different. When she'd finished it, despite her deliberately random strokes across the paper, she could clearly see a definite image of a powerful bird in flight. Most of its shape had been created by the pushing of her fingers around the layers of colour with highlights, here and there, in often unused lighter shades of yellow and pink and white, to pick out an eye, a feather, a talon. She didn't remember creating the bird but there it was, soaring proud and bright and majestic on top of the dark, sticky mess.

What disturbed Mae the most was that it looked beautiful. She couldn't deny it. It was still completely different to all the watercolours and portraits and pictures for sale, but beautiful nevertheless. She didn't understand it, but she knew it was somehow special.

It took all of Mae's strength to tear her eyes from the picture. It was dark outside now and the sickness in her stomach began to feel more like hunger. She remembered then that she hadn't eaten since seven o'clock that morning and perhaps that's why her head felt so light. Was it really that late?

She could stand it no longer. With small, quick movements, Mae jumped off the sofa, picked up the picture, turning it over so that she couldn't see its face, and pulled the old metal trunk out from under the table. She opened it and slipped the picture inside, on top of all the other pictures, and shut the heavy lid down firmly.

She was tired and the room had grown cold, but Mae knew she must eat. She could tidy up the oil pastels and paper afterwards. She walked through to the kitchen, switched on the light and opened a cupboard. There were a couple of tins of tomato soup in there – one of those would be quick and easy and, most of all, comforting. There was a pen sitting on the side under the cupboard. Mae picked it up and paused, still for a moment. Then she went back to the trunk and opened the lid. She'd forgotten to write the date on the picture. All the pictures had been dated. No matter what condition Mae was in after finishing one, she had still made sure they were all dated. She was always slightly uncomfortable about this little ritual because she didn't really know who she was dating them for. Who on earth was ever going to be allowed to see them? She took the picture back out of the trunk and wrote the date in black in the bottom right-hand corner.

Mae looked at the image again. Her eyes were glued to it once more, wondering and confused. Then she did something to it that she had never done to any other picture in the trunk. She gave it a name. She wrote Flight of the Falcon across the top of the picture, took a deep breath, tore her eyes from it, and then placed it face down again on top of all the other pictures.

The trunk was locked tight. Mae went to the kitchen to make some soup. Something had changed. Something new was about to begin.

THE PAIN THING

File Notes Classified at Level B until further notice

COMPARISON REFERENCE – FAUNA
(*From the Biological Institute's archives*)

Every year, from the deep lochs of Ireland, adult eels called 'silvers' make an epic journey across the Atlantic Ocean to the warm, still waters of the Sargasso Sea near Bermuda. They make this pilgrimage purely for the purposes of spawning. After spawning – their last act on Earth – the adult eels die and the tiny eels that are born make the long voyage back to Ireland. If they manage to reach maturity (around eight to fifteen years later), the new adults set off for the Sargasso Sea to begin the marathon cycle all over again.

For centuries scientists wondered how these small creatures navigated across the Atlantic expanse, through all those ocean currents, ships and sonar interference, without getting lost. The answer is simple: The survival of the species depends upon it. To facilitate this, there exists between the still lochs of Ireland and the Sargasso Sea a hidden pathway, specially designed for silver eels to move along. While the eels are on it, the electro-magnetic current of this pathway actually pulls them, minimising the huge effort needed to swim across the Atlantic unaided.

How do the eels know when they've drifted off this invisible road?

It hurts.

Every time the eels drift they begin to experience intense pain - what humans might feel as severe headaches, nausea or extreme anxiety. They feel the pain and start to thrash about in desperation until suddenly the pain stops and they know that they are back on the right path.

This is the consequence of their evolution. They have no choice.

+++++

RELEVANT HISTORICAL CONTEXT
(Extracts from Central Information archives, year 2093)

Of all the different kinds of pain that there are – some natural, some invented so long ago that everyone thought they were natural, some unavoidable, some even manufactured for so-called 'pleasure' – it has now been established that there is one primary reason why humans feel pain: It is to let them know that, whether by accident, momentary lapse of concentration or even wilful stupidity, they are not where they are supposed to be. Pain is the best navigation system that has been developed in the universe so far. It is meant to be brief but ultimately effective. The greater the pain, the more lost the human.

By the start of the twenty-first century, only a small number of humans could remember about the Pain Thing. Understandings and advisories had been written, sung, theatred, danced for as long as it had been necessary to instil pain into the affairs of the human race. These advisories had almost entirely been lost with the destruction of the world's great libraries and sacred places, and the precious little that survived was mostly out of reach of the masses. The memory was so atrophied in the majority of the people at that time, that one or two advisories even existed, in plain view of all but the most isolated humans on the planet, but they were walked past every day without a second glance.

There is more that is yet worse.

Through the centuries of human history since the Pain Thing was introduced, there were those who ignorantly, or deliberately, warped the truth about it. Thereby pain became punishment, and even reward.

There had even been those who wilfully inflicted pain upon themselves, feeling that they were lost and so punishing their own bodies and minds, even sometimes publicly, not understanding that they were pulling themselves even further off the path by their mad self-harm. These were the flagellants. The more they whipped, tore and gouged, the more lost they became. The more lost they felt, the more they beat, gashed and gored, until there was nothing left.

And then there were those, even more grossly misguided, who used pain to punish others in order to distract themselves from their own pain, as if they could exorcise it from themselves by moving it from their own bodies and minds to the bodies and minds of others. Their actions caused such a crescendo of agony on Earth that it became worse than the pain itself – it became anaesthetic, so that they could feel nothing at all.

In the end, the tormented cries of the masses became so great, and the consequences upon the economy so grave, that The Administration was forced to intervene. It must be recorded that this was done at the request, and with the full compliance, of almost all the people on Earth.

Where there had once been pain there was now numbness. The pain of being lost was diluted, made tolerable in a million ways. The best navigation system in the universe, smothered with the thick blanket of not wanting to know, to believe, in case the truth should hurt more than the pain. The irony was that it was precisely the other way around – it was the absence of truth that hurt more than anything else. That was the whole point of the Pain Thing. So, more and more painkillers of all sorts were demanded by the people, and therefore devised by The Administration, just in case anyone should remember.

(Handwritten note transcribed): And there lay the difference between eels and humans. Eels had no desire for anaesthetic. They need to feel pain.

+++++

TEST CASE No. 0004: 'STELLA'
(Female; 28 years old; under observation since April 2107)

Stella can feel pain. By some accident, genetic mutation or perhaps through sheer willpower, she has become immune to the chemical, electro-magnetic, visual and aural anaesthesias that were so successfully introduced by the previous administration.

(Note: three other cases have come to light within the last few days – two in the Northern Quadrant, and one in the East; all of them are female.)

Not only is Stella embracing her immunity to painkillers, she is utilising the subsequent biological and psychological signals for decision-making purposes. This naturally overrides the central decision making databases that were necessarily put in place by The Administration some years ago. This means that Stella has become autonomous in her responses to all external and internal stimuli. The consequence of which being that The Administration is no longer responsible for Stella's choices. This is clearly a serious development, and one which requires a great deal of both scientific and philosophical research. Even the theological may need to be considered.

We have now begun thorough forensic tests on Stella. Perhaps, once we have fully decoded her DNA, we will be able to locate some kind of antidote; a serum that can be used either for the reawakening of the human race or, if that should prove to be too dangerous or too soon, for Stella's own final relief. The decision has yet to be made as to which would be kinder.

AS ABOVE SO BELOW

The depth of the regret commands the grief.
Sweet, precious life, we held you much too brief.
How spiteful short the time we thought we had
to work out how to taste the sane from mad.
Or did we think we figured truth from lies,
instead of looking out through twisted eyes?
Like children on a long, brave summer's day,
had we the curiosity to play?
Like tokens in God's big, bewildering game
of endless repetition, endless pain.
Beyond the bruising, losing, eating chain,
mankind must fill some purpose, have some aim.
Or is it all too vast for us to know?
As above – so below.

As above – so below:
Or is it all too vast for us to know?
Mankind must fill some purpose, have some aim
beyond the bruising, losing, eating chain
of endless repetition, endless pain.
Like tokens in God's big, bewildering game,
have we the curiosity to play
like children on a long, brave summer's day?
Instead of looking out through twisted eyes;
Or did we think we figured truth from lies?
To work out how to taste the sane from mad,
how spiteful short the time we thought we had.
Sweet, precious life, we held you much too brief.
The depth of the regret commands the grief.

WHISPERING TREES

They were selling cheap fruit trees at the corner shop today. A bargain at two for ten pounds. They were young and still small, but the label said they would grow up to five metres. I bought two, an apple and a pear tree, hoping I would live to see them grow tall one day.

When I was young, I used to go to the forest on the edge of the small town where I grew up. I could take the old road, before they widened it, and pedal all the way there on my bike along the thin pavement on the side. At first I went with school friends, racing each other to the forest's edge for prizes we never won and punishments we never received, except in childish words. 'First one to touch a tree is the king of the castle!' 'Last one to touch a tree eats dead rats for dinner!' Then games of tag and off-ground-touch would follow and pocket-money-sweets would be shared. It was our adventure playground, free and with limitless rides. But I fell in love with the trees more than the playtime. I don't think any of the others properly looked at them, ever. We could have been anywhere on the planet, as long as we were away from our parent's beady eyes.

Soon I started to visit the forest alone at times when I knew the others wouldn't be there. First thing in the morning was best, after my mother had gone to work on the early shift at the factory. I'd be the first, and probably the last, to touch the trees on those morning visits, and then I would dash to school to get there just in time to beat the bell. I didn't tell a soul about it. They wouldn't understand.

As the trees became my friends, I began to lose the human ones. I felt myself become distant and different from them, and they felt it too. It came to a head thanks to stupid Harry and his desperate need to show off in front of the girls. One spring afternoon after school we all cycled to the forest again. He beat everyone to our usual spot, threw his bike to the ground and clambered up the big chestnut tree near the pond.

'I'm the king of the castle!' he barked, 'and I need a sword to prove it.' Then, clinging on to the fat trunk of the tree, he began to kick and kick at one of the long branches sticking out at the side. It came away with a high-pitched 'crack' and fell heavily to the ground. With it fell a perfect little bird's nest, three tiny, speckled eggs tumbling out with it onto the earth. Harry cackled deeply and jumped down. 'And now for the king's breakfast,' he said, and stamped all over the eggs until the shells, with all their precious contents, were smashed and scrambled into the dark brown soil.

I flew at the idiot boy in a fury, my arms flailing, shouting the rudest words I knew and screaming that he was a murderer and an evil bird killer. One of my angry, wild fists hit him square in the middle of his face, more by accident than anything else. His nose erupted into a bloody mess and he howled like a banshee. The other boys laughed, a couple of the girls sympathised with me for a moment, but mostly they all just thought I was crazy. The king of the castle burst into tears, crying that I'd broken his nose and swearing that he'd get me back. That's when I grabbed my bike and pedalled out of the forest without looking back.

There was some teasing and name-calling at school for a while, but these things are forgotten as soon as some other childhood trauma or adventure comes along to replace them. I never went to the forest with the others again, but my private morning visits became more frequent and more special.

In the school library was a book called *The Little Book of Trees*. It was a comprehensive guide, with pictures and proper names, that was small enough to fit in my pocket. I stole that book and read it in the forest. When I learnt to recognise a willow or an oak or a silver birch, I would put my hands on its trunk and introduce myself. I'd call the tree by its name and tell it mine. Some of them would invite me to sit under their branches when the sun was strong. Some of them didn't like to be climbed and some were pleased to be embraced.

Some were homes for animals and birds and insects. Some knew how to keep them away for their own reasons. The fauna knew which was which, and soon I did too. You can learn by reading about things. You can learn better by watching and listening. You learn best of all by feeling, although it's hard to explain that to people.

When the summer holidays came around, I didn't have to rush away from the forest so early. I would make a sandwich and eat it under my favourite willow before the others came to play. One day I fell asleep by that tree, deep inside the forest. The sun was warm and the thick carpet of ferns underneath was comfortable and soft. I'm not sure how long I slept, but I was woken by the snap of twigs under approaching feet. I sat up and pushed my stiff back into the trunk of the tree, hoping to hide myself from this intruder in my forest. 'How long was I asleep?' I wondered. 'The others must have come early. They mustn't find me,' and a feeling of panic began to knot my stomach.

A short distance away, among the silver birches, a lone figure was approaching, too tall to be any of my classmates. They saw me as they got closer and headed in my direction. I stood up and brushed the soil and dead leaves from the seat of my jeans. It was a lady, a bit older than my mother and smiling, carrying a willow-branch walking stick and with a blue cloth bag slung over her shoulder.

'Hello,' said the lady. 'I hope I didn't startle you.' Her face was friendly and slightly flushed from walking. Her posture had an ease about it and I noticed her feet were bare. She was carrying a pair of canvas shoes in her hand, which she dropped to the ground along with her bag. Her loose, long hair was dark brown with spangles of silver in it that caught the sun and reflected it back. She smiled at me and I smiled back. 'What's your name?' she asked.

'Ali,' I said. 'This is my forest.' I don't know why I said it out loud like that. I felt my cheeks get hot.

The lady let out a gentle laugh. 'That's funny,' she said. 'I thought this was my forest. My name's Sarah. Can we share it?'

I nodded in agreement and bent to pick up my rucksack. *The Little Book of Trees* tumbled out of its unzipped pocket. I grabbed it and stuffed it back in. I knew she'd seen it. I meant to go then, before I embarrassed myself any further, and definitely before my classmates came and found me with this strange, barefoot old lady. But she stopped me before I could make my excuses.

'I'm just about to have a bite to eat,' she said. 'Would you like to join me? I'd love to talk to you about the trees. I love them too.'

Times were different then. Perhaps people were less suspicious of strangers, I don't know. I'm sure there was just as much reason to be wary as there is now. My mother always told me not to take sweets from strange men, but nobody had ever mentioned barefoot women of the woodlands. My bike was on the ground within easy reach. I was a quick child. If she tried anything, I could easily slip her grasp and pedal away like fury. But I didn't think of any of this at the time. It seemed the most natural thing in the world.

We sat under the willow tree and talked. Inside the blue cloth bag the lady had an old biscuit tin full of homemade flapjacks. I'd already eaten my sandwich, but I took one gratefully all the same. In between mouthfuls I told her all the proper names of the trees I could see, which ones were natives and which ones were evergreen. I pointed out the ones that liked hugs and the ones that didn't, and I told her which ones had secret hollows filled with squirrel nuts and owl's nests. The lady listened and nodded as she nibbled on flapjacks. I talked and talked about all the things I knew and loved about the forest, all the things I had never spoken to a soul about because I didn't think they'd listen, or care if they did. Something about this lady made it okay for me to say it all out loud. She made me feel brave.

When all the flapjacks were done, my talking was done too. 'I'm sorry,' I said. 'I don't usually talk this much. I've never seen you here before.'

'But I've seen you,' said the lady. 'You normally leave soon after I arrive, but you're always in such a hurry that I'm not surprised you've never seen me.'

'I have to run to school in the mornings,' I said, 'but it's the summer holidays now. I can stay here all day if I want to.'

'Won't your parents miss you?'

'No,' I explained. 'My mother works long hours and my father's dead.'

'I'm sorry to hear that,' she said.

'That's okay. I never knew him,' I said. She didn't ask for any more details. I was glad that I didn't have to give any. This wasn't the place for sad stories.

'Would you like to know a secret about the forest?' she asked.

I nodded.

'You talk to the trees, don't you?'

I nodded again and started to pick at my fingernails. What had she seen me do when I didn't know anyone was watching? Had she seen me dancing with the hazel tree? Or whispering to the chestnut tree by the pond? Nobody was meant to know.

'It's okay,' said the lady.

She felt my discomfort and shifted herself around so that I could look into her eyes. I saw then that they were green like the leaves of an elder.

'I've been visiting this forest for many years,' she said. 'I speak to the trees like you do. But here's a question: Did you know that they can talk too?'

My eyes widened as I gazed into hers. I shook my head. This was a secret I didn't know.

'Oh, yes,' she said. 'You can ask questions of the trees and they'll tell you what they know.'

'How?' I said. 'I've never heard them say a thing.'

'That's because you haven't taken the time to listen. You're always having to rush off to school.'

'Not today,' I reminded her.

'That's right. Shall I tell you about it?'

'Yes, please.'

'But not here,' she said. 'Your friends will be arriving soon. They won't be interested at all. Important things like this are only for those who care.'

'They're not my friends,' I protested.

The lady smiled. 'Come with me,' she said. 'It's not far.'

We gathered up our things and walked just a short distance until we reached a big oak behind a row of holly trees. The oak was ancient and it's lower branches hung out and down, forming a wide, green skirt around its thick, gnarled trunk. We settled ourselves down under the canopy. It felt cool and safe in there. I could see through the spiky holly trees to the willow where we'd met. Beyond that I'd be able to spot any intruder classmates without them seeing us. This was a perfect spot. 'Is this where you've watched me from?' I asked.

'Sometimes,' said the lady. 'This is my favourite tree. Do you have a favourite?'

'Yes,' I said. 'It's the big willow tree where you found me.'

'Do you know why it's your favourite?' she asked.

'I don't know. It just feels special, I guess.'

She smiled as if she knew. 'Has it ever occurred to you that the tree welcomed you there? That the willow chose you and not the other way around?'

It hadn't occurred to me at all. But then, I was only nine years old. 'Tell me about the trees that talk,' I said. 'What do they say?'

'They tell you what they know,' she said. 'If you ask them nicely, that is.' She put her hand behind her and felt the trunk of the tree tenderly, stroking it downwards towards the ground. 'How old do you think this oak is?'

I shrugged. 'I don't know. It's very big, so it must be very old.'

'Indeed,' she agreed. 'I'd guess it's at least two hundred years old. Can you imagine what it's seen in all that time? All the people that have sat here or walked by. The bombs that landed on the town during the war. The cars and trucks that thunder down the road over there where once there were horses and carts. The planes that fly overhead, and all the birds and deer that have gone. It can tell you all about those things and more. And maybe one day it will tell someone about you and how you broke a boy's nose for hurting one of its kind.'

'He was mean,' I said.

'I know,' she said.

I tried to listen. 'I can't hear anything. Maybe this tree doesn't want to talk to me. It's your favourite, not mine.'

'You have to be patient,' said the lady. 'You have to wait and listen with your mind, not your ears. The trees don't use words. They speak in pictures. Listen...'

The lady closed her eyes and leant back against the oak tree. She took a deep breath, held it for a moment, then let out a long sigh. I leant back too. I didn't know what to ask the tree. There were too many questions. I heard nothing except the blackbirds overhead and the faint rustle of leaves in the lazy summer breeze. I suppose I gave up too quickly. 'Nope!' I exclaimed. 'I can't hear anything. Maybe I should try this with my willow tree tomorrow.'

The lady opened her eyes and gave me a warm smile. 'It doesn't matter,' she said. 'You can choose any tree you like. That's the second part of the secret. All the trees talk to each other. If you touch one part of the forest, every other part of the forest knows that you're here. And every forest and woodland talks to every other, all around the world.'

'How is that possible?' I said.

She pointed through the leaves of the oak trees hanging branches. 'You see that lime tree?' she said. 'I reckon it's about fifty years old. For all that time, it's stood next to this oak tree. They can't escape each other, you see.'

I didn't see at all. That must have been obvious from the frown that puckered my forehead as I tried my best to understand.

'Imagine being stuck in the same room as another person for the whole of your life; a person you didn't choose to share the room with,' she said. 'You'd have to learn to get along with them pretty quick, otherwise both your lives would be unbearable. You'd have to find a way to be in sympathy with each other, wouldn't you?'

'I guess so.'

'And that's how it is with the trees. That's how it's been for millions of years. They understand that they're all part of the same thing. They're all children of the forest.'

The lady reached out a hand and took an oak leaf from the nearest branch. She twirled it around in the air with her fingers. As the sunlight shone through, I could see its pale-coloured veins spreading out to the tips, like streams branching out from a river. 'That, my dear, is how the trees speak to each other. You tell one leaf your secrets, and you tell the whole forest.'

Just then we heard a clattering noise approaching from the direction of the road. It was the other children on their bikes, coming to waste some time and make a mess in the woods. 'Oh, no,' I sighed. 'They're here. Do you think they'll see us?'

'They've never noticed me before,' said the lady. And they didn't notice this time either.

The summer seemed long that year. I found the lady in the forest many times. She taught me all the names of the birds and which trees they liked to nest in. She brought flapjacks in a tin, and I brought cookies that I'd learnt to bake at school. Sometimes we'd sit under her favourite tree, and sometimes we'd sit under mine. She would ask questions of the forest and wait for the answers. I waited too, but I never heard a reply. Not for many years, anyway. Then the summer ended and I had to go back to school. I never saw that lady again. Perhaps she saw me. I don't know.

These days I'm all grown up. My home town and the forest are far behind me. In the end, my classmates and me discovered that there were few opportunities for us in a small town. One by one, we all left for the cities and the jobs and lives that they could offer.

It's taken me twenty years, but I've finally managed to save up for a place of my own. A ground-floor flat with one bedroom and a garden that's all mine. It's an overcrowded part of the city. It's hard to hear the blackbirds over the cars and the drills and the people, but at least I have a garden. I couldn't live without one. When I moved in, it was just a blank patch of grass with some ivy climbing over the high brick walls, but I've been planting lavender and mint in the hope that it will grow wild around the borders and cover up the smell of petrol fumes.

Today I bought two fruit trees from the shop on the corner. An apple and a pear. They were a bargain at only ten pounds for two. They're young and small now, but one day they'll be five metres tall. I hope I live long enough to see them mature.

I'm going to plant them next to each other in the middle of the lawn. I know they'll get along. They'll have plenty of sunlight and water and I'll talk to them every day. I'll tell them all the secrets that I can't tell anybody else. I'll ask them to send a message to the willow and the oak tree in my forest back home. I'll ask them to tell them that I'm still here, and I'll listen for when they send a message back to me.

DUSTMAN

A half-moon reclined in the soft of the night,
Resting, relaxing and sharing its light
With the people of Wendon, a city so great
That its streets were quite clean and its trains never late.

Among the fine folk of this urban idyll,
Was a chef of great fame and immeasurable skill,
For his food was renowned, his dishes applauded,
His culinary wizardry amply rewarded.
But tonight he just wept in a darkened alley,
Outside the back doors of his restaurant, 'Chez Me'.
He cried and he sobbed and kept calling out, 'Why
Do I feel so bereft? Am I living a lie?'

'Can I help?' asked a dustman, both smiling and wise.
Chef sat up, surprised by the light in his eyes,
For he'd been so absorbed in the depths of his gloom,
That he hadn't yet noticed this man and his broom.

'Can I help?' he repeated, he was not dismayed.
'No, you can't,' sobbed the chef, 'for I am beyond aid.'
'Let me be the judge,' said the dustman, 'Alright?'
And he sat by the chef who then told of his plight.

'Food is my life', said the chef of himself,
'It's the be-all and end-all and source of all wealth
And light to the soul...' he paused to sigh deep,
'But the light has gone out and I can't seem to keep
From feeling suppressed and depressed about what
Could have stolen my love of the spoon and the pot.'

'I can help,' said the dustman, 'but I need your trust.'
'I've tried,' wept the chef. 'It has all turned to dust.'
'Once more, I can help, and will, if you choose.'
Chef shrugged, then a nod; there was nothing to lose.
'Just find me great food, that's all that I need.'
And the dustman stood boldly and told him: 'Agreed!'

With one hoist of his broom to his shoulder he strode
Out of the alley and down to the road.
The chef walked behind with his head hanging down,
As they walked through dark streets and out of the town.

They carried on walking through village and glen,
Down valley, up hillside, then village again.

They walked and they walked, then walked a bit more,
Past rivers and lakes, past cliff face and shore;
Past steeples so tall and pastures pristine,
Over pavement and cobble and smooth village green.

As the sun rubbed his eyes the chef lifted his head,
'How much further to go? I am hungry,' he said.
'Have faith,' said the dustman, and carried on walking,
'I think you should save up your strength by not talking.'
For a night and a day they walked on in this way,
Till at last they arrived in a dark alleyway.
By now the poor chef had a ravenous hunger,
'Please sir,' he enquired, 'Must we walk any longer?'

The dustman first found an old box for a seat,
Then asked of the chef, 'Are you ready to eat?'
Chef could but nod and sit down not too far
From the curious stranger who'd brought him this far.

From his pocket the dustman produced a neat package
All wrapped in brown paper – a single cheese sandwich.
The chef stared in wonder, then took a small bite,
His eyes shone with joy, he cried, 'What a delight!
I have never known food so delicious before,'
And he savoured each mouthful with reverence and awe.

The dustman then asked, 'Will you drink with me?'

As he poured from a flask a small cupful of tea.
'What nectar is this?' cried chef with one taste,
And he drank with great care in avoidance of waste.

'I'm cured!' said the chef, 'My hope is repaired,
Thanks to this marvellous feast you've prepared.
My great love of food is not lost anymore,
You have given me back the one thing I adore,'

The dustman looked on as the chef danced with glee;
'It's important that you understand this,' said he:
'Love cannot be lost, no matter how small.
You forgot what it is to be hungry, that's all.'
With that the wise dustman bade chef a good night,
Picked up his broom and walked into the night.

Chef understood, and from then to this day,
His deep love of food never has gone away.

THE POET & THE STARGAZER

(One day I was fascinated to discover that William Shakespeare and Galileo were born just a couple of months apart in 1564. Perhaps they met somewhere one day. Perhaps they had a conversation. Perhaps it was something like this.)

'Why must you spend your time staring outwards into the universe?' said the Poet to the Stargazer. 'Do you not see that there is an expanse of equal importance waiting to be explored inside a man?'

The Stargazer sighed and shifted his weight to the back of his chair. He pulled at the whiskers on his chin. 'And which man might this be, my friend?'

The Poet leaned forward in earnest and replied, 'Not simply a man, but any man.'

'Ah!' said the Stargazer, '*Anyman* is a different beast altogether. I must admit that I have never met a man so ignorant that I could not learn from him.' He paused briefly to let the Poet know he might have something further to say of importance, then changed his posture to match that of his companion. 'But you mistake my actions, dear fellow. It is not the universe I stare into, but God himself.'

'That explains much,' the Poet responded. 'I see why the Church condemns you so fiercely. If you tell them that you stare at God through a telescope, they will hang you for a heretic before you can calculate that two plus two makes four.'

The Stargazer let out a snort of disdain. 'The Church!' he cried, 'I would no sooner speak of God to the Church as I would speak mathematics to a herd of swine. They despise me for blasphemy and force my silence.'

'Do not mistake their motives,' the Poet said with knowing. 'The Church hates only what it fears, and what it fears is your voice, should you choose to set it free.'

'But I am not a wordsmith as you are,' the Stargazer protested, 'I am a man of science and thinking.'

The Poet, with a patient look said, 'Be careful now, it is dangerous to think too much in times such as these,' and paused before continuing. 'But being a thinker, think: if you do not speak your revelations, how will the world be changed? For if something is not written, it simply does not exist.'

The Stargazer stared back and frowned. He said, 'You expect me to throw my dearest discoveries into penny plays for the tickling of the masses?' And further he added, 'You speak of talk and words as if they are the only tongue, but mathematics is the language with which God has written the universe.' And there the Stargazer folded his arms as if he had won some great tournament.

'Now you mistake *me*,' the Poet protested, 'I stare into God as you do, but I can speak him to any man. I have learnt that the best place to lay a truth is within a sigh or a speech, a tickle or a tear, for love is love and hope is hope for both queen and serf. As human feelings are the same for all, so must truth be; and that, my friend, is my philosophy.'

The Stargazer smiled. He enjoyed this regular jousting, and he was warming to his companion more than ever. He rose and moved to the table by the window. He uncorked a bottle and poured out two glasses of his best wine. 'Fine words,' said he, passing a glass to his eager companion. 'Fine words, and intelligently spoke, but perhaps we could have the humility to agree that there are more things in heaven and earth, dear Poet, than are dreamt of in our philosophies.'

The Poet laughed and raised a glass to his friend. 'There we must agree and see that we are not so different. But I fear now,' said the Poet, 'that you have stolen my line.'

THE MIRACLE OF CAMDEN TOWN

A miracle happened today. I was in my usual spot by the entrance to the tube station. That's where I sit, that's where I sleep, where I think. It's where I do everything. I've been here for three months. It's been a long three months too, but I can't go back where I came from. I've got to go somewhere else, but up until this morning it felt like I was going nowhere and taking forever to do it. Anyway, I want to stay in the up side because a miracle happened today.

I was just sitting there. The clock in the station said that it was half past ten in the morning. It was cold so I had my sleeping bag wrapped round my legs to try and keep the chill of the pavement off me, and I was watching, like I do. It was packed with all the people pouring into Camden to hang around the market, sit in coffee bars and do whatever normal people do on a Saturday. I can't remember what that's like anymore.

It's funny, you know. One of the worst things about sitting here and never meeting people - I mean, not *really* meeting people. Or at least no-one you'd want to meet - is that you only get bits of conversations as they walk past. You never hear the end and you never hear the beginning, you just get bits, and sometimes you really want to know where a story came from and where it's going to. Sometimes I just want to chase them up the road and say, 'Hey! What happened next?' but I never do. That's what my life is like. It's like watching a party going on through a dirty window. Wanting to do something but never doing it.

Sometimes someone chucks me fifty pence or a pound. Or those that don't want to encourage people like me but feel really guilty about it, they'll drop a little something to eat or drink into my lap, a sell-by-date sandwich or a hot cup of tea. I don't ask for it. I just sit here. I don't ask. If I did, I'd say, 'I don't like egg mayonnaise. Can I have something else?' But I don't. This guy said to me once, 'It will be easy for you 'cos you're a girl and you're young. You'll get sympathy from the guilty ones, especially the women. It's even better if you've got a dog.' I'd like a dog, but I don't want the responsibility. I was told I can't handle responsibility. That's one of the reasons I'm here.

People stop looking at you when you live on the street. Perhaps I mean seeing, not looking. You become invisible really quick. I sometimes think I could do anything in this doorway. I could take all my clothes off, stand on my head, I could do anything and no-one would look. No-one would see. But I've never tried it, just in case.

Then today a lady talked to me, and she really was a lady. Do you know how I knew she was a lady? Because she looked me right in the eye, not stooped over me or looking down at me, but she crouched down in front of me and looked me straight in the eye with this proper, warm smile on her face. She had the same colour hair as my mum, dark brown and curly and poking out under her hat and over her collar. She didn't mind coming down to where I was and she said, 'Hello. Chilly today, isn't it?'

And I said, 'Yeah, it is.'

Then she took off the blue, woolly gloves she was wearing and held them out to me. 'Put these on,' she said. 'They're still warm.' And they were. Then she said, 'Take care of yourself.'

And I said, 'I will.'

She smiled again and put her hands inside her pockets. They must have been cold already. 'It will get better, you know,' she said.

That's when the miracle happened. I said, 'I know.' Just like that, I said, 'I know,' and I believed it. I really believed it deep down inside. I felt it from the top of my head to the tip of my freezing cold toes. I smiled then too.

The lady pulled her hand out of her pocket and there was a couple of pound coins and some change in it. She put the money into my gloved hand. 'Get yourself something hot to drink. It will help to keep you warm.' Then she walked away down the road. I watched her until she disappeared inside all the crowds of people, moving up and down the high street like a thousand worker ants. Then I couldn't see her anymore.

I told the truth to that lady, just like I felt it. I do know, deep down. It's got to get better, hasn't it?

THE FIRST ISLAND

It was seven months after all the birds had died. It was three months after all but basic communication had been silenced. That was when the big wave hit the East Coast. All of the remaining trees had been on that side, and the wave washed the stumps and shattered debris that was left into the sea. Tsunami Number Four had originally torn the flora and the buildings from their roots and foundations, and now even those had been sacrificed to the ever-deepening water. All that remained on the last island were a few gnarled tendrils of roots, rusty pipes and twisted girders. They all poked out of the starched earth like broken fingers searching for something to grab hold of.

The last island had been a heavily populated part of a once great continent. Now it was raised in areas that once were flat, and submerged in other places to be half-remembered as some vast, mythical Atlantis. Now there was only one limitless blue ocean, stretching out from all sides of the island and all the way back around the planet. It was dark and deep, and empty of all but the toughest, hard-shelled marine creatures and the scattered, sea-buried remains of billions of years.

Natasha opened her eyes and felt the sting of salt in them, the salt that the sea had left behind. Her fingers were dry and cracked like the tree roots, frozen into claws from clinging to the stonework of the last monument's pedestal. She uncurled one hand slowly and rubbed the other with the rough skin of her palm.

The monument groaned in the briny wind that rolled across the island in waves. Natasha decided it was time to move now before it fell like all the others. It was a miracle that this one had lasted so long. Her clothes were drenched with dirty water, and she felt the wet linen of her dress sticking to her skin as she rose unsteadily to her feet. The wind was cooling the cloth quickly and drying the salt into patches of hard, sticky crystals. Her impulse was to remove all her clothes, but it was cold.

'Mona!... Winston!... Alfie!' Natasha called the names of the last survivors she could remember, but her mind went blank after the first three. In any case, the names were swallowed up in gusts of wind; ripped from her cracked lips as soon as she opened her mouth.

She called again: 'Winston!... Alfie!... Mona!' She thought she heard some sound come back but couldn't be sure. It might have been the humming of the sea. It wouldn't take long to search the shrinking island, and that's what Natasha felt she must do. She moved just a second too late. The creaking from the stone pedestal turned into a deep, gravel roar as the giant copper structure on top finally gave way. It fell in sad slow motion, in a wide, graceful arc towards the ground. Natasha felt her own weak structure groan, her bones complaining loudly as she threw herself away from the toppling giant.

It had taken fourteen years, more than a century before, to construct the imposing statue – created as a beacon of hope for a world that had been extinguished in only seven months. The name of the artist had long been forgotten. As the monument fell, it created a wide cloud of smoke and dust and copper splinters that covered almost a third of the island. Natasha's miscalculation meant that her left foot was trapped under the very edge of the statue's debris, the tip of a giant forefinger pinning her to the wet ground.

A century of history now hung as nothing more than dust in the air, filling Natasha's nose and mouth with the thick taste of wet copper and burnt wood. It tasted like blood, and she coughed the worst of it out of her mouth before attempting to call out again.

'Mona!... Winston!'

With each call, her voice became more of a croak, but this time there was a reply and some definite movement to the left of her narrowing vision. A man, some years younger than her, was carefully making his way towards Natasha on his hands and feet, like some cautious ape. As he crawled closer, she wondered what colour hair the man had underneath the thick covering of grime that had settled all around them. Later she would recall this as an odd thought to have under the circumstances. 'Winston?'

'No. My name's Lewis. Don't move.'

Natasha rubbed some fresh dirt from her eyes and looked at the picture around her. Fine particles of ash and debris were falling quickly to the ground, pushed down by the water still hanging in the air. Lewis had moved to Natasha's trapped foot and was digging with his hands into the wet, muddy ground beneath. Natasha watched as if she wasn't there; as if she was watching the whole thing take place on some foggy playback screen; as if she was back on the leather lounger in her apartment, watching some late-night movie.

Lewis dug deeper. 'Is it broken?' he asked.

'What?'

'Your foot – is it broken?'

Natasha wasn't in her apartment anymore. It had gone, with all the other buildings, by the time Tsunami Number Three had hit. She snapped back to the present but could feel nothing except the blood-like taste in her mouth. 'No, I don't think it's broken. I can move it.'

Lewis finished digging a neat hole, just big enough to slide Natasha's foot out from under the giant forefinger. As she did so, Lewis settled back against the metal and coughed some dust out of his mouth, too. 'Were you alone?'

Natasha looked around at the settling haze and the flattened remnants of glass, metal and stone that lay all about her, mixed now with mud and sea salt. 'There were some others. I don't know if they made it. I was going to try and search the island.'

'Yeah, we could do that.' Lewis brushed the worst of the dust from his head and Natasha saw then that his hair was brown. 'I was making my way up to that ridge to get a better view. Looks too dangerous now.' Lewis pointed to a newly formed hill, made up of lumps of twisted metal that had once been cars.

'Where were you? In the sewers?'

'No, no. They flooded out pretty quick. There was a big tree stump down near the river. I don't know how I held on, but the wave passed much quicker than the last one. I'm gonna try to get up there.' Lewis motioned to the top of the central part of the statue. A large portion had fallen intact, and giant folds of metal fabric provided a natural pathway to what was now the highest point on the island.

Lewis climbed and Natasha followed. The old, pock-marked copper covering was easier to climb than it looked, and they were both at the top in a few minutes. The wind had started to drop and they found a dip in the contours of the monument where they could sit in relative comfort.

For the first time, Natasha took a good look around. 'Oh, my God!'

'What is it?'

'I had no idea it would be beautiful.' Natasha looked at the ocean that stretched before them on all sides. The waves had settled into gentle, regular ripples that stretched out in long lines for miles. Way off in the distance, further than she had ever been able to look so far, there was a bank of dark, grey clouds spattered with lightning. Above their heads, the clouds had started to break and shafts of sunshine were falling all around. The contrast was magnificent. The only sounds were the lapping of the waves on the shore of this new island, and the occasional creak as the wreckage settled into itself.

Lewis turned his head slowly, scanning the broad horizon. 'Yeah, I guess it really is beautiful.' He felt in his shirt pocket as he scanned the scene. He found a crumpled pack of cigarettes and a small box of matches, amazingly still dry. 'Can you believe these babies survived?'

Natasha turned to see Lewis's precious spoils, tilted her head back and laughed. She hadn't laughed for a long time and it took a while to stop. Lewis laughed too. It was infectious. Once they managed to catch a breath, he pulled out a cigarette for each of them, and struck the match sharply on the green-blue metal where they sat. It burst into a tiny flame on the third strike and he cupped a hand round the precious fire to protect it from the wind.

The first inhalation caused them both to cough up smoke and bits of dust out of the bottom of their lungs, and they smiled with satisfaction at each other once the coughing had subsided. They looked out at the ocean, sharing their cigarettes like old soldiers after battle.

Lewis broke the silence first. 'What's your name?'

'Natasha. Natasha Hamlock.'

'Good name.'

'Thanks. I always liked it.'

'Did you think it would be this quick?'

Natasha paused, blowing out a neat column of smoke. 'Nope. I thought we had years.'

The wind had dropped to a cool breeze and the sun was now shining all across the island. Way out in the distance, the lightning illuminated the dark clouds in bursts. Natasha became aware of the wet fabric around her body again and shivered slightly.

'Would you mind too much if I took my clothes off?' she asked. 'I just really, really need to get dry. This wet dress is making me cold.'

'It doesn't bother me, and who else are you gonna offend?'

'Thanks.' Natasha carefully placed her cigarette on a dry piece of statue and began to peel the wet layers of clothing from her tired body. The warming sun felt good on her skin, and she took up the cigarette again and relaxed. Lewis did the same, and the two naked strangers sat on the monument's folded garments like Greek athletes at some ancient Olympic games.

'Are these the last of the cigarettes?'

Lewis checked inside the packet. 'There's two more left.'

Natasha nodded with a smile and their silence resumed. There were no birds or other people. The only sound was the pat of waves lapping against the island.

'I used to be an architect,' Natasha said wistfully.

'No kidding! I was a plumber. We hated you guys!'

'Yeah, I know.' And they laughed again. 'When you design a building,' she said, 'you have to have an image in your head of exactly what it's gonna look like in the end, before you even start. Then all you have to do is draw what you see.'

'Hard to design a building for this place right now. Did you see *this* image in your head?'

'No. If I'd have seen this, I would have built something different.'

'I just didn't think it would be this quick,' said Lewis, flicking away his cigarette butt and rubbing his face with his hands, 'No warning; nothing that we took seriously, anyway.'

They looked out across the water. Time had stopped ticking. It might have been five minutes or an hour before Lewis took his eyes off the hypnotic movement of the sea to begin scanning the ground of the island. Most of what had once been on the surface of it was unrecognisable; the rubble of buildings mixed with the shells of cars and sea creatures, the remains of TVs and computers and sofas and dead birds. And dead people. 'I don't think there's anyone else left.'

Natasha glanced around the island, then chose to look back out across the water instead. 'I'm surprised that we're left.'

'If there's no-one else left, I guess these last two cigarettes are ours.' Lewis took the bent, white sticks out, crumpled up the pack in his hand and threw it off the top of the statue.

The bright red and white cardboard stood out like a rare jewel against their grey, black and brown surroundings until it fell out of sight into the mud.

The second match lit first time, and the wind had now dropped enough for the flame to stand up easily on the tip of the wooden shaft. Lewis inhaled deeply on his last cigarette and blew a ring of smoke out towards the ocean. 'I've been trying to give these up for months.'

Natasha smiled. 'Do you think if they'd have known, they would have bothered to ban smoking in public places?'

'Hell, yeah! They had to keep us busy arguing about something.' Lewis sat back a little further into the statue's folds and felt the goose pimples flatten on his flesh as the sun warmed his skin. 'Do you think they knew?

'Who?'

'The guys who sold gasoline and fired rockets in the air, collected the taxes... And banned smoking!'

'You mean the billionaires and the politicians?'

'This is no time for politics.'

Natasha laughed. It was good to feel it in her belly.

'Seriously, though,' Lewis pressed. 'Do you think they knew that something like this was going to happen?'

Natasha took a long drag on one of the last two cigarettes in the world. 'Didn't we all know?'

FALL

Dropped from the big tree,
Gliding like lost birds in winter,
I try to catch the leaves; waiting, ready,
Trying to guess which one will fall down next;
Anticipating sudden disconnection;
Light but violent end of usefulness.
But over and again it's one behind or out of reach
That tumbles through the air
To join the pile of yellow, dry decay
That floats like froth on top of blackened seas.
As each one falls it weaves
Into a magic carpet at my feet;
Rich in red and yellow-brown,
Slow breathing in and out to match the earth,
Knit so close I can't remember which fell last.
And in my hand, after an hour or more, is only one,
And on the ground a thousand more are joined,
Sinking in slow motion, deep into the soil.

Why do we fight so hard to grip the end of things?
As if by closing tight our hand
We keep them from their death.
When all we ever have to do
To stop a thing from dying
Is open up our hand and let it fall
Into the start of something else's life.

I open up my hand and look
At one dry, yellow leaf.
And underneath the weeping birch I stop
And drop something I thought was dead so it can live.

THE AMBER LIBRARY

When the last regime had finished burning the books, I went to look in secret places for any that they might have missed. I went with Frank and Elsa and Ray, because four sets of eyes are better than one.

They always miss some of the books. Sometimes they are the best ones, if you know how to recognise them. Oppression is bad at detail. It wields its authority like a hammer and suppresses in big lumps with no discretion. That's why they never catch the small things. That's why they never succeed in the end. Another regime will try when this one fails, and they will fail in their turn. That's how it's always been. That's why we went looking for the books in secret places.

The last book we found was in the back room of a bombed-out bicycle shop. There it was between boxes of bike chains, burnt a little around the cover but still readable amidst the rubble. The flames had eaten the name of the author but the title still remained: *For Those Who Are Yet to*

Come. As they always say, you can't judge a book by its cover, but clearly this was a dangerous piece of literature. Maybe that's why someone had hidden it. It seems they didn't survive to retrieve it. Their work was done all the same. We found it for them and for the future and we were grateful to the stranger who had time to hide it. Elsa opened her large canvas shoulder bag and slipped the book inside with the others we had already found. Then me and her and Frank went to Ray's place to read.

Ray lived in a sixth-floor apartment on the industrial side of town. His neighbours were mostly essential workers from the building trades who worked long hours. They kept to their own business, relieved to have jobs that meant wages and food. Ray was smart. When the tanks first rolled in and the university was destroyed, he borrowed a pair of overalls and moved quietly from his professor's digs to this anonymous block of flats.

The streets were becoming dark when we got there. Only one or two windows at the top of the block were illuminated. They wouldn't see us from up there. Everyone else was probably still at work. There was a lot of rebuilding to do.

Ray let us in to his one large room that served as kitchen, living room and bedroom. We could relax here for a while in relative safety. 'I'll put the kettle on,' said Ray. 'I expect we could all do with a hot drink.' He motioned to me. 'You get the Amber Library. You know where it is, don't you?'

I nodded and went to fetch what he'd asked for. Ray lit the gas stove and put the battered tin kettle on it to boil. In the corner of the room beside the front door was a row of coat hooks, covered with jackets and hats. On the floor underneath was a large wooden crate with the word 'TOOLS' stencilled on its grubby lid. I opened the crate and ran my fingers around the edge of the wide, shallow tray that sat at the top. It was filled with a random assortment of old hammers and planes and rusty nails, clearly mismatched and unused for years. Ray had found them by the rubbish bins outside, discarded by his neighbours as no longer useful. They served only to disguise what lay beneath. My fingers found the small gaps in the side of the tool tray and I lifted it out and placed it heavily on the floor. I got out the precious contents from the bottom of the crate and carried it to the kitchen table.

The Amber Library was a box made of hammered brass with a solid oak bottom and a beautiful lid made of amber-coloured glass. In the centre were a few well-chosen pieces of real amber, set in the shape of an open book, and around this, all the various segments of glass were etched with images of leaves and flowers and insects. When the lid was opened and held in front of a window, the light would shine through it so that the whole thing glowed with an ancient kind of warmth. The box had been presented to Ray at the university for an achievement long forgotten, rendered insignificant by the bigger events that had happened since. He himself never spoke about his accolade, but it was the one precious thing he had brought with him from his rooms at the university. As Ray would often say himself, it now housed something far more precious than any medal or award. It was where we hid all the important books that we could find among the wreckage of our city. He said the books inside would be like bee wings in amber - preserved fragments of knowledge for future times.

Elsa opened the lid of the Amber Library. Inside were a dozen volumes, some intact, some partly damaged. There was easily room for two dozen more. She fetched today's haul from her canvas bag; five new additions, including the last one that we'd found in the bicycle shop. This was the one we wanted to see first. The title was irresistible: *For Those Who Are Yet To Come*.

When Elsa pulled back the charred cover, we saw that only the first page of the first chapter was still readable. The rest was more badly damaged than we had first thought. We closed the curtains, lit a few candles, and huddled together around the kitchen table. We decided that Ray would read out loud. He had the best voice for it. He cleared his throat, held the book out with care and read:

'Freedom cannot be courted but it must be won; won because it was lost a long time ago. It is won by removing everything that is not freedom. This is easier said than done, but done it must be otherwise this existence is an expensive waste of time.

Freedom exists where there is nothing in the way that can stop it. It flows like water and can move around and over anything that is not sealed shut in front of it. Any opening can provide a channel for freedom, as long as it's not full of sludge – then freedom does not come out but muddy water does. This might move like freedom, but it smells and tastes like effluence. Don't be fooled. Taste it first. If it tastes like fresh air, it might just be freedom.

Taste is not the only way to tell; there's feel too. Freedom feels like pipes being blown by giants. It feels like the lightness of dreams. If it feels like you can hold it in your hand, then it's not freedom – taste it again.

Then if you're sure that it tastes right, and it feels right, then look to see where it sits. If it's written on your shoes or the front of your shirt, then it's not freedom. If it's in your wallet or hanging on the wall, then it's not freedom. If it walks with you or is there at your side when you stand up, then it might just be freedom – taste it again.'

That's all there was. Ray put the book down on the table and took a long, deep breath. None of us spoke for a minute or two. Then Elsa asked him to read it again. We listened to the words as Ray recited them more slowly the second time. Elsa read it aloud the third time by way of an experiment. A female voice might reach our insides in different ways, speak to other parts of us. Precious things are worth the time.

When she'd finished, Elsa put the book down on the table again. No-one spoke for a long time. We shared the silence. We knew that we would have to write the rest of the book ourselves.

ACKNOWLEDGEMENTS

Nothing is created from nothing. Something has to be put in before you can get something out. Without the help and support of the following people, it would not have been possible to produce this book. This is a perfect opportunity to set my gratitude down forever in black and white.

Thank you to my husband and chief editor, AJ Deane. He wields his red pen without flattery or mercy, and always with one aim: to help me be the best writer I can be. His belief in me has never wavered, nor mine in him. The best is yet to come.

Thank you to my mother. Without her generous support, I would never have been able to publish my first book. And without that first book, I would never have had the confidence to continue.

Thank you to my friend of thirty years and counting, Andrea Kennard. Her wonderful photographs have graced my book covers, and her generosity for allowing me to do as

I will with them has shown me great trust and generosity. I am always inspired by her beautiful work and blessed with her friendship.

Thank you to Valda Fisher and Huw Chapman at Waterstones, for championing me from the start and making me feel like a real author, even before I was one!

Lastly, thank you to my fellow authors and companions who have been there with advice, support and encouragement throughout pandemic lockdowns when our creativity and resilience was greatly tested. I hope I have provided you all with as much strength as you have given me. Thank you: Justin Newland, Rachel Churcher, A.E. Warren, Julia Blake, MT McGuire, and Marjorie Mallon.

We are all in this together!